A Page to Panto script
by
Joe Meloy

Robin Hood
A pantomime in 2 acts

First Published in Great Britain in 2023 by Beercott Books.

Copyright: © Joe Meloy 2023

ISBN:978-1-7393020-4-7

www.beercottbooks.co.uk

Beercott

For Ashley Kemp,
my best mate,
love you always.

MAIN CHARACTERS

ROBIN HOOD

MAID MARION

NURSE NELLIE SCARLET - (Dame)

SILLY WILLY SCARLET - (Comic. Also, part of the Merry Men)

SHERIFF OF NOTTINGHAM

FAIRY DEWDROP

ALAN-A-DALE - (part of the Merry Men)

FRIAR TUCK - (part of the Merry Men)

LITTLE JOHN - (part of the Merry Men)

JACK

JILL

MINOR ROLES

TOWN CRIER

KING RICHARD

NUTS - (Pantomime Horse)

CHORUS ROLES

VILLAGER 1

VILLAGER 2

VILLAGER 3

CHILD 1

CHILD 2

CHILD 3

GUARD 1

SCENES

ACT 1

PROLOGUE - Front of tabs

SCENE 1 - Sherwood Market

SCENE 2 - Sherwood Forest

SCENE 3 - Nurse Nellie's Bedroom

SCENE 4 - The Kitchen

SCENE 5 - Sherwood Market

SCENE 6 - Sherwood Forest

SCENE 7 - Marion & the Babes Bedroom

SCENE 8 - Sherwood Forest

ACT 2

SCENE 1- The Sheriff of Nottingham's Lair

SCENE 2 - Sherwood Forest

SCENE 3 - The Sheriff of Nottingham's Lair

SCENE 4 - Sherwood Market

SCENE 5 - In Front of Tabs (Songsheet)

SCENE 6 - Bows

PROLOGUE

IN FRONT OF TABS

(Overture)

FAIRY: Good evening, everyone
          And welcome to the tale we've just begun
          We've got the good and the bad
          I'm here to help the good or else we'll end up sad
          We've got a dashing hero, Robin Hood
          Defender of the bold, the brave and the good!
          There's a nasty villain, a horrible man
          And of course you must boo and hiss his evil plan

(Enter SHERIFF OF NOTTINGHAM)

SHERIFF: *(Evil Laugh)* Did somebody mention my name?
          Oh, look at this audience it's such a shame!
          You're here to see me in all my glory
          This isn't about Robin Hood this is my story!
          I can see you're all such a big fan
          I happen to be Prince John's right hand man

FAIRY: When King Richard returns, you'll see!

SHERIFF: Ha! King Richard has nothing on me! He'll never return
          from the crusades

FAIRY: King Richard will return and your power will fade!

SHERIFF: Oh, shut up you tiresome Fairy!
          Your words they do not scare me!
          I'll raise the taxes through the roof

FAIRY: Why must you be so Uncouth!

SHERIFF: Nonsense everybody loves me, oh yes they do!

FAIRY: Oh no they don't!

SHERIFF: Oh yes they do!

FAIRY: Oh no they don't!

SHERIFF: Oh yes they do!

FAIRY: Oh no they don't!

SHERIFF: Oh, this is ridiculous! I'm off, catch you later losers! *(Evil Laugh. Exit)*

FAIRY: What an absolute brute!
Never mind him it's time to sing, dance and have a hoot!
Now our story is about to begin, let's go to Sherwood
Where the party is in full swing!

SCENE ONE

SHERWOOD MARKET

Song One – MAID MARION & Villagers

MARION: I do love singing and dancing with you all!

VILLAGERS: Thanks Marion etc

MARION: I'm so looking forward to the town fayre this week, with all its stalls of delicious food, hook a duck, splat the rat and of course the annual archery contest!

NELLIE: *(From offstage)* Yoo-hoo!

MARION: That sounds like Nurse Nellie

(Enter NELLIE)

NELLIE: Oh, hello everyone!

VILLAGERS: Hello Nellie etc

VILLAGER 1: Where've you been Nellie?

NELLIE: Well, I've been to the deli

VILLAGER 2: The deli?

NELLIE: Yes, I saw a programme on the telly about the deli

VILLAGER 3: That's amazing Nellie!

NELLIE: Oh my what a day me Nurse Nellie first watching the telly, saw a programme about the deli, that was selling something smelly-

MARION: Something smelly?

NELLIE: Yes, something smelly at the deli from the telly for me Nurse Nellie.

VILLAGER 1: What was smelly from the deli, you saw on the telly Nellie?

NELLIE: Cheese.

VILLAGER 2: Cheese? Was it from the deli up the hill?

NELLIE: Yes when walking up the hill I had to give it some wheelie, to get to the smelly deli, from on the telly, to get the cheese for me Nellie!

VILLAGER 3: That sounds like quite the day!

NELLIE: Well, that's not the half of it! After the deli, I felt a rumble in my belly!

MARION: You must have been hungry!

NELLIE: I'll say I must have built up an appetite, giving it some wellie, to get to the smelly deli from the telly to get some cheese for me Nellie to fill my belly!

VILLAGER 1: So, you've already eaten the cheese?

NELLIE: Not quite I rather fancied some jelly instead

VILLAGER 2: Some jelly, did you get that from the deli?

NELLIE: No luckily, I bumped into an old friend Kelly who had just made some.

VILLAGER 3: Kelly made some Jelly?

NELLIE: Yes. So, I gave it some wellie to get to the smelly deli from off the telly to fill my belly then I bumped into Kelly who knew me Nellie and gave me some jelly.

MARION: Hasn't Kelly got a twin sister?

NELLIE: Oh yes Ellie who was with Kelly when I got the jelly.

VILLAGER 1: What about their Mum?

NELLIE: Oh, you mean Shelley yes, she was there as well with Kelly and Ellie

VILLAGER 2: Sounds like you've had a packed day!

NELLIE: Yes, I have. I gave it some wellie to get to the deli that I saw on the telly to buy something smelly, to fill my belly then I bumped into my old friend Kelly and her sister Ellie who gave me some jelly and as I left I passed their Mum Shelly, who said 'Hello Nellie, where have you been?' and I said 'I've just been to the deli' and she said 'the one from the telly' and I said 'yes the deli from the telly' and she said 'climbing up that hill you must have had to give it some wellie' and I said 'I did give it some wellie to get to the deli from off the telly to get something smelly' and she said 'did Kelly give you some jelly to fill your belly' and I said 'yes both Shelly and Ellie gave me jelly to fill my belly' and she said 'well I'll see you soon Nellie' and I said 'Ta-rah! Shelly!'

MARION: Can you say that again?

NELLIE: Not a chance! Haven't you lot got things to be getting ready for the fayre this week?

VILLAGERS: Yes etc

NELLIE: Well go on then off you go!

VILLAGERS: Okay Nellie, bye Nellie etc.

NELLIE: *(Noticing the audience)* Oh, Hello boys and girls! I'm sure we can do better than that! Hello everyone! That's much better! What a lovely looking lot we've got in tonight! Honestly, you're the best audience we've had in tonight!

Well, how silly of me boys and girls I haven't introduced myself my name is Nurse Nellie Scarlet and I'm Mother to Will Scarlet one of Robin Hood's most loyal and trusted merry men! Though we all call him Silly Willy Scarlet! Because he's well… You'll see when you meet him! And I'm also the Nurse to Robin Hood and the rest his Merry Men if any of them get a bobo they come and see me. I can treat the mumps, the bumps and all of the above!

I do love living in Sherwood apart from when that horrible Sheriff's about. Have you met him yet? Oh, isn't he horrible he makes Maggie Thatcher look like a saint in comparison!

Mind you that Robin Hood's a cheeky one and as for his Merry Men they might be even cheekier, but I can't help loving them all!

Though saying that two of the Merry Men got caught stealing last week! Little John stole a selfie stick, I told him after that he needed to take a long look at himself. And Alan-a-Dale stole a board game, he said it was worth the RISK.

And last week Friar Tuck stole an iPhone, I told him he could face time… And then there's my boy Will he misunderstood when Robin said they were going to loot Curries… He came back with an arm full of chicken tikka masala!

Now boys and girls I've made a very special Trifle for the fayre this week and I'm going to leave it over here *(places the trifle stage left)*. Now if you see anyone sneaking up on my trifle, I need you to shout Nellie! As loudly as you can, can you do that boys and girls? Well, can you? Right let's give it a practise go then *(NELLIE sneaks up to the trifle)*. Well did you do it? I didn't hear anything! You'll have to speak up I'm deaf in one eye! *(NELLIE sneaks up on the trifle again)*, that was a bit better, but you need to be louder I could be all the way in Sherwood Forest! *(NELLIE sneaks up on the trifle again and this time the audience are loud enough)* Oh! That's much better! They probably heard that all the way in *(insert local reference here)*! Right, I best be off I need to go and find my son now where is that Silly Willy Scarlet! Bye bye boys and girls! *(Exit NELLIE)*

(Enter SILLY WILLY SCARLET crashing on)

WILL: Hiya boys and girls! Come on I'm sure you can be louder than that! I said Hiya boys and girls! My name is Will Scarlet, but people often call me Silly Willy Scarlet because well- I'm a bit silly! I'm one of Robin Hood's Merry Men and we're always stealing from the rich to give to the poor people of *(insert local dive here)*.

Robin's away at the moment but he should be back soon, he never goes away for too long! I'm sure you'll meet him very soon, then again if you didn't meet him, it'd be a bit of a cop out, I mean his name's all over the poster!

Hey, hang on a second boys and girls would you all like to be part of the Merry Men as well? Would you? Oh brilliant! In that case then every time I come on I'm going to shout 'How are you all feeling!' and you'll all shout back 'Merry!' Come on let's give it a go! 'How are you all feeling!' *(Merry!)*. Come on you can all be louder than that! 'How are you all feeling!' *(Merry!)* Third times the charm; 'How are you all feeling!' *(Merry!)* That's fantastic! Now you're all officially part of the Merry Men!

Now I wonder where the rest of the Merry Men are, they were supposed to meet me here ages ago!

Song Two – WILL SCARLET & THE MERRY MEN

(Song Ends and ROBIN HOOD enters)

ROBIN: Ah my Merry Men! How good it is to see you all!

JOHN: Welcome back Robin!

TUCK: Yes, welcome back Robin, how was your trip?

ROBIN: It was great, but it's getting even harder to dodge that horrible Sheriff of Nottingham!

ALAN: Do you know he's put the rent up again!

ROBIN: Again?

TUCK: If he puts it up again no one will be able to afford to pay their rent and they'll be out on the street!

ROBIN: We'll help them out! We'll steal from the rich, to give to the poor like we've always done!

ALL: *(Cheer etc)*

WILL: Hang on is that a trifle over there!

TUCK: I do love a good trifle!

(All move toward the trifle. Audience: Nellie!)

(Enter NELLIE)

NELLIE: Who's trying to steal my trifle! Oh, I might have known it'd be you lot! You lot stay away from my trifle!

ROBIN: Sorry Nellie!

NELLIE: Now I've got a question for you lot! How comes when I woke up this morning someone had stolen my fairy liquid, my washing up powder and fabric softener?

ROBIN: I don't know Nellie-

WILL: But it sounds like they made a clean getaway!

NELLIE: Oh Will, you silly boy!

TUCK: Oh, Nurse Nellie actually I've got something to show you-

NELLIE: I've told you Tucky if you keep putting the cream on it, it'll go away!

TUCK: No not that! This *(Whistles, a pantomime horse enters)*

NELLIE: I see you've bought a horse! What's it's name

JOHN: Nuts!

NELLIE: What an odd name!

WILL: We've taught Nuts some tricks Mum!

NELLIE: Go on then show me a trick

WILL: Nuts dance! *(NUTS does a little dance)*

NELLIE: That's marvellous what else?

ALAN: Nuts sit *(NUTS farts and a poo falls out)*. No I said sit!

NELLIE: What do you feed him?

JOHN: Peanuts! *(NUTS using a water gun pees at the audience)* No Nuts! Bad horse! Bad horse!

WILL: I think that's quite enough for one day. Off you go nuts! *(Exit NUTS)*

NELLIE: What an extraordinary creature! Right come on you lot I think it's dinner time!

ROBIN: Can you put mine on the side Nellie, I'm going to go and see Marion first! I haven't seen her in what feels like forever!

NELLIE: Very well Robin! See you later *(Exit MERRY MEN and NELLIE saying bye Robin etc as they leave and ROBIN exits the opposite side to NELLIE and the MERRY MEN)*

(Blackout)

SCENE TWO

SHERWOOD FOREST

(Enter MARION)

MARION: I wonder where Robin could be… Hey! What's that trifle doing over there! *(Goes toward trifle. Audience: Nellie!)*

NELLIE: *(entering)* Who's after my trifle! Oh, Marion it's only you. Say what are you doing waiting out in the forest all by yourself?

MARION: I'm waiting for Robin.

NELLIE: Have you not seen him yet?

MARION: No, have you?

NELLIE: Yes- *(walks over to MARION in some discomfort)*

MARION: What's wrong Nellie, you look like you're in some pain.

NELLIE: I was out shopping a couple of days ago and tub of margarine fell on my foot. I can't believe it's not better.

MARION: Oh Nellie, I'm sure it'll feel better soon!

NELLIE: But it's not all bad news I was doing the shopping last week and there was a naked man running around-

MARION: Was it Lidl?

NELLIE: I don't know I didn't have my glasses on!

MARION: Where is Robin, he said he'd be here by now.

NELLIE: I'm sure he'll turn up-

ROBIN: Were you talking about me, the one, the only, the very dashing, Robin Hood!

MARION: Robin! *(They embrace with a hug)* I'm so glad you're back!

ROBIN: *(Said with MARION in his arms)* In every moment of danger, I thought of you Maid Marion and how I had to get back to see you again! *(ROBIN turns to NELLIE as if to gesture her to leave. NELLIE instead nods back at him and smiles oblivious).* Hadn't you better be going now Nellie?

NELLIE: No, I'm actually enjoying the fresh air-

ROBIN: Still a nice night for a walk though.

NELLIE: I prefer to stand here and gaze up at the stars.

ROBIN: I think they might look better down by the lake.

NELLIE: No. I'm fine here honestly.

ROBIN: Nellie, please leave.

NELLIE: Oh, I see how it is… *(Hamming it up being sad)* I'll just leave then. *(Exits)*

MARION: Oh Robin!

NELLIE: *(Re-enters very quickly. Sings.)* All by myself-

ROBIN: Yes, thank you Nellie!

NELLIE: *(Hamming up the sadness once more)* It's alright I know when I'm not wanted-

ROBIN: Correct you're not wanted-

NELLIE: What a dreadful thing to say to a woman

ROBIN: That's pushing it.

NELLIE: I'll have you know many a man has fallen at my feet-

ROBIN: They must have got a shock when they looked up!

NELLIE: Oh, you cheeky young man. Fine I'll go! *(Exits)*

ROBIN: Finally.

NELLIE: *(Re-enters very quickly again. Sings.)* Lonely, I am so lonely, I have nobody to call my own-

ROBIN: Nellie please!

NELLIE: Yep. Fine. Sorry. I'll leave you two alone. A man and a woman. Alone together both very much in love, having not seen each other for months. Oh no wait, now I get it. *(Pause)* See you later Robin. *(Exits)*

ROBIN: Finally we can-

NELLIE: *(Re-enters very quickly again and walks across the stage)* Sorry I went off the wrong way! *(Exits)*

ROBIN: I love you Marion.

MARION: And I love you!

> *Song Three – ROBIN & MARION*
>
> *(ROBIN & MARION kiss. Blackout)*

SCENE THREE

NURSE NELLIE'S BEDROOM

(NURSE NELLIE is fast asleep. Enter FAIRY.)

FAIRY: Jack and Jill are next in line to the throne
And I must find them a happy home
The babes will now appear for me *(Waves her wand)*
This will be a safe place for you to be
The Sheriff wants you both dead
So he can place the crown on Prince John's head
But fear not for here in this den
With Marion, Robin and the Merry Men
You'll be safe and sound
Until King Richard's ship touches ground

(NURSE NELLIE wakes up and sees the FAIRY and starts to scream)

NELLIE: There's a man in my boudoir! Help, help Robin, Merry Men! Save me-

(Enter ROBIN, MARION and his MERRY MEN at great pace with their bow and arrows and swords drawn)

FAIRY: Stop I am no man! I am a Fairy
There is nothing in this land less scary!

WILL: How are you all feeling! *(Audience: Merry!)* Brilliant! Oh, wow a real life Fairy! I've always wanted to meet a Fairy!

NELLIE: Careful son that's how I started!

FAIRY: Now listen one and all-

NELLIE: Do you have to speak in rhyme? It gets very confusing!

WILL: Yeah, you could always speak normally if you wanted too!

FAIRY: *(Breaks into a cockney accent)* Thank goodness for that I was getting so tired of rhyming everything. The other day I ended a sentence with the word orange. I was stood there for four hours trying to figure out a rhyme!

WILL: That's much better! Now tell us Fairy- erm Fairy- What's your name?

FAIRY: I am Fairy Dewdrop!

WILL: Fantastic! Very well then Fairy Poo Plop-

NELLIE: That is not what she said William Scarlet! *(Clips him round the ear)*. Fairy Dewdrop do continue.

FAIRY: Thank you. These two kids here are called Jack and Jill and they're next in line for the throne and the Sheriff of Nottingham is after them so he can get rid of them-

TUCK: Get rid of them?

FAIRY: *(Gestures that the SHERIFF will kill them)* So the crown goes straight to Prince John!

MARION: What a horrible man. Don't worry children you're safe here with us.

ALAN: Yes, we'll look after you both

TUCK: You'll love it here!

JACK & JILL: Thank you!

FAIRY: Jack and Jill must stay here hidden until King Richard returns.

NELLIE: Don't you worry, under our care we'll see that that nasty Sheriff of Snot-ing-ham never finds them! And as soon as King Richard is back, we can tell him all about what the Sheriff has been up too!

JACK: Yeah, and that horrible Prince John as well!

JILL: Then they'll both get their comeuppance!

FAIRY: Right, I've got to go.

JOHN: Are you off to help someone else with your Fairy magic?

FAIRY: No. Love Island starts in twenty minutes. Now remember look after those kids!

MARION: We will Fairy Dewdrop. We Promise don't we everyone!

ALL: Yes of course we do etc

FAIRY: Thank you all for your help. Ta-rah for now! *(Exit FAIRY)*

ROBIN: Right then I think we need to find somewhere for you two to sleep.

MARION: Come on everyone let's show Jack and Jill around!

ALL: Great idea, yes lets etc

(They all exit it off escorting JACK and JILL)

SCENE FOUR

THE KITCHEN

(Lights up on NELLIE & WILL who are in the kitchen)

WILL: How are you all feeling! *(Audience: Merry!)* Great!

(Enter ROBIN)

ROBIN: Ah Nellie, Will there you both are!

WILL: Here we both are!

ROBIN: Now today we I need you two to make dinner for the Merry Men.

WILL: But we don't know how to cook!

ROBIN: That's alright you can simply follow along to the cookery show on the radio.

WILL: What are we making?

ROBIN: Let me just put the radio on to find out! The cooking show is just about to start.

(ROBIN tunes in the radio. That is placed on the other side of the stage from NELLIE and WILL)

RADIO COOKERY PRESENTER: Hello and welcome to cooking with me Barry Cooksalot. Today we'll be making a lovely meal that all the family can enjoy!

ROBIN: There we go perfect. Now just do everything they tell you to do. *(Exit ROBIN)*

WILL: You've got it Robin!

RADIO COOKERY PRESENTER: First you'll need a mixing bowl.

WILL: *(Holds up mixing bowl)* Got it!

RADIO COOKERY PRESENTER: Then you'll need some flour and eggs.

NELLIE: *(Holds up the eggs)* Got them!

RADIO COOKERY PRESENTER: And of course, you'll need plenty of water!

NELLIE: There's no water. Come on let's go and get some. *(Exit NELLIE & WILL)*

(Enter MARION with a watering can and gardening tools)

MARION: I simply must spruce up the garden, it's looking a right state!

(Tunes the radio to the gardening programme)

RADIO GARDENING PRESENTER: Hello and welcome to gardening time with me Bobbie Dandelion

MARION: Hang on I've forgotten my hose!

(Exit MARION. Enter NELLIE & WILL from the opposite side of the stage. It's important that during this scene NELLIE and WILL always enter from the opposite side from everyone else, so that they can't see the radio being re-tuned)

RADIO GARDENING PRESENTER: Now then first things first make sure you have everything!

WILL: Yep, we've got everything!

RADIO GARDENING PRESENTER: Now then take your gloves and put them on

NELLIE: We haven't got any gloves!

WILL: We'll have to go and find them!

(Exit WILL & NELLIE. Enter LITTLE JOHN & FRIAR TUCK)

JOHN: I'm telling you Tuck, you listen to this radio show about keeping fit and you'll be ready to run that five K in no time!

(JOHN tunes the radio to the sports channel)

RADIO SPORTS PRESENTER: Hello and welcome to keep fit with me Maisy Jogs-about.

TUCK: I've forgotten my trainers!

JOHN: We best go and get them.

(Exit JOHN & TUCK. Enter NELLIE & WILL)

RADIO SPORTS PRESENTER: Now you're ready it's time to begin. Let's start with some star jumps.

WILL: What's that got to do with cooking?

NELLIE: It's like when you warm the oven but instead, we're warming up the cooks!

WILL: Well, that makes sense.

(Enter ROBIN who tunes the radio back to the cookery show without WILL & NELLIE seeing him, whenever someone comes onto re-tune the radio WILL & NELLIE remain completely unaware)

RADIO COOKERY PRESENTER: Now let's get the flour in the bowl.

(NELLIE & ROBIN frantically put all of the ingredients into the mixing bowl, apart from the water. Enter MARION, who re-tunes it to the gardening show)

RADIO GARDENING PRESENTER: Now it's time to use some water, don't be afraid to use plenty of water.

(NELLIE tips the jug of water in the bowl)

RADIO GARDENING PRESENTER: You'll need plenty of water you'll find it easier to apply the water with a hose.

WILL: We haven't got a hose.

NELLIE: *(Takes out two super soaker water pistols)* No, but we have got these.

RADIO GARDENING PRESENTER: Now don't be afraid to really get the water everywhere.

WILL: Everywhere?

NELLIE: That's what he said.

(WILL & NELLIE squirt water all over the audience. Enter ROBIN who tunes the radio back to the cookery show.)

RADIO COOKERY PRESENTER: Now you've used just enough water to moisten the bowl. It's time to put the eggs in.

NELLIE: Eggs, where did we put the eggs.

(NELLIE & WILL search for the eggs. JOHN Enters and changes the radio to the sports channel)

RADIO SPORTS PRESENTER: Now throw them up in the air.

NELLIE: What?

RADIO SPORTS PRESENTER: That's right throw them back and forth and be careful not to drop them!

(NELLIE & WILL throw the eggs back and forth to one another)

RADIO SPORTS PRESENTER: Now try one on your head.

WILL: Okay. *(WILL throws an egg in the air and heads it)*

RADIO SPORTS PRESENTER: Great stuff now if you have a friend there with you have them throw one at your head.

NELLIE: You don't have to ask me twice! *(NELLIE throws an egg at WILL'S head)*

(Enter MARION, who changes the station back to the gardening channel and exits)

RADIO GARDENING PRESENTER: Now that you've got that everywhere. It's time for you to get your feet involved. Really get your feet stuck in and stamp it down.

WILL: Okay *(Take the bowl and stamps in it with his feet)*

RADIO GARDENING PRESENTER: Really go for it. Jump up and down and really flatten it down.

(WILL jumps up and down in the bowl. Enter ROBIN who changes the station back to the cookery channel and exits)

RADIO COOKERY PRESENTER: Now by this point you should have a nice dough. Now roll into a ball

NELLIE: Oh yes! We've got a lovely ball of dough.

RADIO COOKERY PRESENTER: Now go and preheat the oven to two hundred degrees Celsius.

(NELLIE & WILL go over to the oven. Enter JOHN who tunes the radio back to the sports channel)

RADIO SPORTS PRESENTER: Now it's time to use our exercise ball.

JOHN: Brilliant! *(Shouting he goes off)* Get the exercise balls Tuck! *(NELLIE & WILL haven't heard any of this as they've been fiddling with the oven)*

RADIO SPORTS PRESENTER: Now place your ball on the floor and sit on it.

NELLIE: I beg your pardon.

RADIO SPORTS PRESENTER: Sit on your ball and roll around to get your balance.

NELLIE: Very well. *(NELLIE sits on the ball of dough and rolls around on it)* I don't see how this is going to make this taste any better.

(Enter Robin who changes the radio back to the cookery channel)

RADIO COOKERY PRESENTER: Now your dough is ready for the oven. Put it in the oven for the next forty-five minutes and wait.

(NELLIE & WILL put the dough in the oven)

WILL: What now Mum?

NELLIE: Well, I suppose we wait.

(NELLIE & WILL sit down and wait a beat before the oven starts to smoke)

WILL: *(Sniffs)* Mum, can you smell burning?

NELLIE: No. Besides if there was something burning this lot out here would tell us *(pointing to the audience)*, but they've not said anything.

WILL: Oh, we must be fine. *(The audience should start shouting about the smoking oven by now, if they haven't WILL & NELLIE can adlib as necessary to get the desired reaction).*

NELLIE: Oh, look fire! There's a fire! *(Sirens start sounding and the stage and auditorium is filled with everyone tending to the fire. Squirting water everywhere running into the audience! All ending with NELLIE going to chuck a bucket of water at the oven but missing and getting WILL instead)*

(Enter ROBIN)

ROBIN: What's happening with dinner?

NELLIE: I think we'll order in tonight!

(Blackout)

SCENE FIVE

SHERWOOD MARKET

SHERIFF: Come on everyone it's time to pay your taxes!

> *Song Four – SHERIFF OF NOTTINGHAM, ROBIN, MERRY MEN, NELLIE and MARION*

SHERIFF: *(NELLIE goes to leave)* Not so fast you lot!

WILL: Hang on a second. How are you all feeling? *(Audience: Merry!)*

SHERIFF: Stop with your absolute nonsense and pay up!

WILL: We're not paying you a penny you big meanie! *(Stamps on the SHERIFF'S foot who then hops about in pain)* Come on everyone leg it!

> *(Chase scene through the audience, during which when they get back to the stage leaving just NELLIE and the SHERIFF)*

SHERIFF: Everyone else might have run off but that means you'll just have to pay everyone's tax! *(Aside)* I'll get the money from this stupid woman I'll simply use my charm and woo her… Hello there my good lady.

NELLIE: Who me?

SHERIFF: Who else would I be talking too?

NELLIE: I know who you are, you're that mean, horrible, nasty Sheriff!

SHERIFF: My dear woman I am none of those things, for I am merely misunderstood. I only collect taxes, for I myself am very poor, if you could spare me some money, I'd be forever grateful…

NELLIE: Well I haven't got anything for you-

SHERIFF: Now listen here you stupid woman I've tried to be nice!

NELLIE: Have you? Because from what I can see you've been fairly horrible-

SHERIFF: SILENCE!

NELLIE: Oh, isn't he butch!

SHERIFF: Right, that's it come here! *(Grabs NELLIE)*

NELLIE: Oh, you have a very firm grip-

SHERIFF: Shut up and hand over your taxes

NELLIE: Well how much do you want?

SHERIFF: I want a hundred pounds!

NELLIE: One hundred pounds?

SHERIFF: Yes, or else!

NELLIE: Oh, fine here you go… *(counting it into his hand)* one, two- I say you do look rather young for your age

SHERIFF: And how old would you say I was?

NELLIE: Not a day over twenty-one, *(counting the money into his hand)* Twenty-two, twenty-three- Go on tell us how old are you really?

SHERIFF: I'm actually fifty-five

NELLIE: *(Counting into his hand)* fifty-six, fifty-seven, and I'm having a bit of a silly moment here if you're in your fifties that must mean you were born in the sixties?

SHERIFF: Yes I was, the year of sixty-eight in fact-

NELLIE: *(Again counting into his hand)* Sixty-nine, seventy- And let me ask you a difficult question what year you were aged thirty-one

SHERIFF: Let's see I would have been thirty-one in… ninety-nine

NELLIE: *(Counting into his hand)* One hundred. A pleasure doing business with you. Bye *(hurries off)*

(BLACKOUT)

SCENE SIX

SHERWOOD FOREST

(Lights Up on WILL sitting alone onstage. Enter NELLIE)

WILL: How are you all feeling? *(audience: Merry!)*

NELLIE: Oh, Will there you are!

WILL: Well, I don't think I'm anywhere else-

NELLIE: Now listen here Will we've not got any money left. We're completely out of cash.

WILL: But we were supposed to order in tonight!

NELLIE: It's alright I've got a way for us to make some money!

WILL: How's that?

NELLIE: Well, what we'll do is bet people that this part of the forest has an echo-

WILL: But it doesn't have an echo.

NELLIE: I know so we'll create one-

WILL: How do we create an echo?

NELLIE: *(copying WILL)* How do we create an echo?

WILL: That's what I just said

NELLIE: That's what I just said-

WILL: No really that's what I just said. There is no echo.

NELLIE: No really that's what I just said. There is no echo.

WILL: Hang on!

NELLIE: Hang on! I'm creating an echo

WILL: I'm creating an echo

NELLIE: No, I'm creating an echo

WILL: No, I'm creating an echo

NELLIE: No really, I am the echo. I'm copying you.

WILL: No really, I am the echo. I'm copying you.

NELLIE: So, do you get it?

WILL: So, do you get it?

NELLIE: No do you get it?

WILL: No do you get it?

NELLIE: Stop now!

WILL: Stop now!

NELLIE: I'm warning you!

WILL: I'm warning you!

NELLIE: I'm going to whack you one in a minute!

WILL: I'm going to whack you one in a minute!

NELLIE: Seriously stop it!

WILL: Seriously stop it!

NELLIE: I will whack you!

WILL: I will whack you!

NELLIE: *(Clips Will round the ear)*

WILL: *(Clips Nellie round the ear)*

NELLIE: What did you do that for?

WILL: You said to copy you!

NELLIE: Yes, only what I was saying!

WILL: Oh, right so I'm the echo!

NELLIE: Yes, you're the echo! Quick someone's coming, go and hide over there and you repeat everything they say.

WILL: Okay! *(Hides behind a tree)*

(Enter ALAN)

ALAN: Good morning Nellie!

WILL: Good morning Nellie!

NELLIE: *(aside to WILL)* Not yet!

WILL: Not yet!

NELLIE: Stop it

WILL: St- *(NELLIE interrupts WILL very quickly)*

NELLIE: Good morning, Alan. Lovely day isn't it!

ALAN: It certainly is Nellie.

NELLIE: Did you know this part of the forest has an echo?

WILL: Did you know-

NELLIE: Yes, it does but not yet it doesn't.

ALAN: Well, I've never heard an echo when I've been here.

NELLIE: What would you say to a little wager then?

ALAN: A wager?

NELLIE: Yes, I bet you ten pounds that the next thing you say you'll hear an echo?

ALAN: That sounds like an easy ten pounds to me you're on!

NELLIE: Go on then shout something and see if there's an echo.

ALAN: Echo!

WILL: Echo!

ALAN: How are you?

WILL: How are you?

ALAN: *(to NELLIE)* Well I never.

NELLIE: Ten pounds please!

ALAN: Very well *(hands over ten pounds and exits)*

WILL: *(Jumping out from his hiding place)* Wow! That was brilliant Mum! Ten pounds!

NELLIE: Quick someone else is coming! *(WILL hides behind the tree again)*

(Enter BIG JOHN)

JOHN: Morning Nellie!

NELLIE: Morning John, lovely day isn't it!

JOHN: Yes, it is rather pleasant.

NELLIE: Did you know there's an echo in these parts of the forest?

JOHN: An echo. No there isn't!

NELLIE: Care to make a little bet?

JOHN: Yes fine! I bet you ten pounds there's no echo in this forest!

NELLIE: Very well, go on then. Say something and see what happens.

JOHN: Hello

WILL: Hello

JOHN: Is there an echo?

WILL: Is there an echo?

NELLIE: Ten pounds please!

JOHN: Fine! *(Hands NELLIE ten pounds and exits)*

WILL: *(Jumps out from his hiding place)* Wow! Another ten pounds! This is brilliant!

NELLIE: I can hear someone else coming! *(WILL hides behind the tree again)*

(Enter SHERIFF)

SHERIFF: *(To the audience who should be booing)* Oh shut up you bunch of losers! *(Noticing NELLIE)* Ah you! I want a word with you, you seem to have diddled me earlier on out of the tax money!

NELLIE: Well, I'll tell you what then we'll go double or nothing!

SHERIFF: Double or nothing?

NELLIE: Yes, I bet you that there's an echo in this forest!

SHERIFF: There's no echo in this forest I have ridden through it many times on my horse and never once heard an echo!

NELLIE: Then surely, it's a pretty safe bet! If there's an echo, we'll call it quits-

SHERIFF: And if there isn't an echo?

NELLIE: I'll pay you every penny I owe you plus next year as well!

SHERIFF: Well in that case then you're on!

NELLIE: Go on then say whatever you want, and they'll be an echo!

SHERIFF: Hello!

WILL: Hello!

SHERIFF: That's impossible!

WILL: That's impossible!

SHERIFF: Oggy, Oggy, Oggy!

WILL: Oi, Oi, Oi

SHERIFF: Oom Pah, Oom Pah!

WILL: Stick it up ya jumper!

SHERIFF: Charcoal, Charcoal!

WILL: Stick it up your-

NELLIE: No! You can't say that!

WILL: *(Comes out from behind the tree)* But you said to be an echo!

SHERIFF: *(Spotting WILL)* Ah Ha! I knew there was no echo!

WILL: What do we do now Mum?

NELLIE: *(Goes over to the SHERIFF)* Hey what's that there? *(Pointing to his shirt. SHERIFF looks down and NELLIE flicks him in the nose and the SHERIFF falls backward)* Leg it!

WILL: See you later everyone!

(Exit NELLIE & WILL at great pace. Blackout)

SCENE SEVEN

MARION & THE BABES BEDROOM

(Lights up on MARION, JACK & JILL who are all asleep in their beds)

SHERIFF: Hello losers did you miss me? Oh yes you did! *(Audience: Oh no we didn't!)* Oh yes you did! *(Audience: Oh no we didn't!)* Oh yes you did! *(Audience: Oh no we didn't!)* Oh, shut up! So then here we are at the secret hideout, did you really think those stupid Merry Men and that idiot boy Robin Hood could hide the true heirs to the throne from me! And look we have a bonus the beautiful Maid Marion, I think I'll take her for my bride! So, here's the plan. I'll take Jack and Jill and leave them in the forest and let the wolves have them, and then I'll marry Maid Marion and live happily ever after! *(Evil Laugh).*

Wakey wakey Jack and Jill it's time for a trip with your dear old Sheriff!

JACK: We're not going anywhere with you! You creep!

JILL: Yeah, you stinky bum!

SHERIFF: Me a stinky bum? Well, I've never been so insulted in all my life!

JACK: Really? I can try again if you want!

SHERIFF: Why you horrible little brat! Just you wait!

JILL: Marion!

(MARION wakes up)

MARION: You what are you doing here! As soon as Robin finds out-

SHERIFF: It'll be too late, you and I shall be wed, and you two miserable little children will have been left out in the forest for the wolves! And then the power and rule of the country will be all mine!

MARION: You'll never get away with this!

SHERIFF: That's where you're wrong my dear! *(Draws his sword)* Now you're all coming with me!

MARION: I don't think so! *(Pulls a sword from under her bed)* Engarde Sheriff!

SHERIFF: You want to fight me? Very well have it your way! *(A sword fight ensues where the SHERIFF gets the better of MARION, knocking her sword out of her hands)*

SHERIFF: You silly little girl thinking you'd get the best of me! Now come along dear we have a wedding to plan! *(SHERIFF points his sword at MARION, JACK AND JILL)*. Now as I said come along all of you nice and quietly. *(Exit SHERIFF, MARION, JACK and JILL. The SHERIFF lets out an evil laugh as he walks them off)*

(Blackout)

SCENE EIGHT

SHERWOOD FOREST

(TUCK enters and has a look around and licks his lips)

TUCK: That trifle does look rather tasty! I'm sure Nellie won't mind! *(Sneaks towards the trifle. Audience: Nellie!)*

NELLIE: Oi! Hands off my trifle! Oh Tucky! It's you!

TUCK: Well, you know I do love a trifle! Particularly your trifle Nellie!

NELLIE: Mr. Tuck are you trying to seduce me?

TUCK: Nellie I can no longer hide my feelings for you!

(A random person walks across the stage with a bell in their mouth ringing it. NELLIE and TUCK watch in silence as they walk across the stage ringing the bell with their mouth)

TUCK: Who was that?

NELLIE: No idea, but her face rings a bell!

TUCK: Now where was I. *(The sound of something falling is heard and the stage gets darker)* What was that?

NELLIE: Nights fallen! Remember when I said earlier the jokes don't get any better… Yeah, I wasn't lying.

TUCK: *(His phone starts to ring he gets it out and goes to answer it only for a famous song to start playing)*. It always does this *(Bashes buttons on his phone)*

NELLIE: *(Phone still playing music)* Why is your phone singing?

TUCK: I don't know.

NELLIE: Let me have a look! *(Takes phone from TUCK the phone is still playing music)* Oh I can see the problem, it's a Sam-Sung phone!

TUCK: Enough of these silly jokes there's something I need to tell you! Can I get a drum roll please *(a drum is rolled onto stage)*

NELLIE: Yes, Tucky what is it?

TUCK: Well, you see, I- I

NELLIE: Yes, Tucky tell me! Tell me everything that's in your heart! *(She pulls TUCK directly into her breasts)*

TUCK: *(Pulling away for air)* I need you to know that- *(NELLIE pulls him in once again)*

NELLIE: Yes, go on Tucky! Tell me everything!

TUCK: *(Pulls away again)* I can't, I can't say it out loud! For every time I go to tell you what I want to tell you I get all tongue tied! I'm going to have to sing it instead!

Song Five – TUCK & NELLIE

(Song ends just as they're about to kiss an alarm starts to sound. WILL runs on at great pace, followed by the MERRY MEN. There is complete panic and chaos everyone is running around like headless chickens in a blind panic)

WILL: How are you all feeling? *(Audience: Merry!)*

NELLIE: What's with the alarm?!

WILL: Marion, Jack and Jill are gone! We think the Sheriff has taken them!

TUCK: Oh no! *(Joins in running around in a panic)*

NELLIE: What are we going to do!

ALL: *(Run around screaming and panicking until the FAIRY appears and the alarm sound stops).*

FAIRY: *(Shouts to get everyone's attention and as she does, they all freeze and the alarm stops. The FAIRY is still not rhyming and speaking in her cockney accent)* OI! NOW EVERYBODY JUST CALM DOWN!

Right, now that I have all of your attention. Jack and Jill have been kidnapped by the Sheriff of Nottingham and he also intends to take Marion as his bride!

ROBIN: That crook!

ALAN: We've got to stop him!

TUCK: But how?

FAIRY: To be honest I don't really know, I've just given you the information-

NELLIE: Some Fairy you are!

FAIRY: Relax I can use my magic to show you where they are!
(Waves her wand. The SHERIFF appears with MARION in a

split scene and JACK and JILL appear in a separate scene tied up in the woods) The Sheriff has Marion at his lair in *(local dive)-*

NELLIE: Do we have to go there?

WILL: Even the pigeons are rough there!

FAIRY: And the babes are deep in the depths of Sherwood Forest, you've got to find them before the wolves do!

ROBIN: Fine then that's what we'll do! We'll find the babes and rescue my beautiful Maid Marion!

Song Six – ROBIN, FAIRY, MERRY MEN and NELLIE

(Blackout)

(End of Act One)

ACT TWO

SCENE ONE

THE SHERIFF OF NOTTINGHAM'S LAIR

Song Seven – SHERIFF OF NOTTINGHAM

SHERIFF: Welcome back losers everything is just as I want it. Those bratty children have no doubt been eaten by the wolves by now and of course I haven't forgotten about my beautiful bride! Guards! *(Two guards bring on a tied-up MAID MARION).* Now my dearest future wife we must talk about our upcoming wedding-

MARION: I'll never marry you, you pig!

SHERIFF: Nonsense you'll come around to the idea of loving me.

MARION: Oh no I won't!

SHERIFF: Oh yes you will!

MARION: Oh no I won't!

SHERIFF: Oh yes you will!

MARION: Oh no I won't!

SHERIFF: Oh yes you will!

MARION: Oh no I won't!

SHERIFF: Oh, be quiet all of you! I can't wait to tell Prince John that he's next in line for the throne.

MARION: He'll never be King!

SHERIFF: You're far too loud for my liking! I prefer my wife only to be seen and not heard! Now where was I… Rumour has it that King Richard isn't doing very well in the crusades, so soon he shall be no more, and Prince John will become King and I will have ultimate power!

MARION: You'll never have total power Robin Hood will stop you!

SHERIFF: *(Mimicking MARION)* Robin Hood will stop you! *(Evil laugh).* Now Marion will you do me the honour of being my bride?

MARION: I've already told you. No, I won't.

SHERIFF: Just know that it pains me to do this-

MARION: Do what?

SHERIFF: Guards, take Marion away to the dungeon. Maybe a few days down in the rat-infested dungeon will change your mind! *(MARION is dragged away by the guards)*

MARION: Just you wait! You'll get your comeuppance! *(Exit MARION and GUARDS)*

(Blackout)

SCENE TWO

SHERWOOD FOREST

(JACK and JILL are tied up back-to-back centre stage. Enter ROBIN)

JACK & JILL: Robin!

ROBIN: *(Untying them)* Jack, Jill it's so good to see you! I'm glad I got here before the wolves did! Where is Marion?

JACK: She's up in the Sheriff's lair. He told us that he's going to marry her!

JILL: And he's a big stupid poopy head!

ROBIN: He certainly is!

(Enter WILL and NELLIE)

NELLIE: Jack, Jill there you are!

WILL: How are you all feeling? *(Audience: Merry!)*

NELLIE: That horrible Sheriff. Leaving you both out here!

WILL: Yeah, wait until Robin gets his hands on him then he's in trouble!

NELLIE: I'm glad we found you both, but we've all been walking for hours!

WILL: I'm soooo tired!

JACK & JILL: Us too!

NELLIE: Yeah, that's because we've been walking for ages, and we're now lost.

ROBIN: We're not lost!

WILL: Then what are we?

ROBIN: Diverted! We can't give up though we still need find Marion!

JACK: I know you can do it!

NELLIE: Well, we best hurry up as it's starting to get dark.

JILL: I don't like it when it gets dark!

NELLIE: Me either!

JACK: And I've heard that this forest is haunted!

NELLIE & WILL: Haunted! *(They grab one another)*

ROBIN: Yeah, by ghosties and ghoulies!

NELLIE: Oh, I'd hate to be grabbed by the ghosties!

WILL: And I'd hate to be grabbed by the ghoul- ghosties as well!

NELLIE: I'll tell you what, why don't we sing a song to calm us down and this lot out here will tell us if they see anything spooky! Won't you boys and girls! *(Ad lib as needed)*

Song Eight

(A GHOST comes behind them and starts to wave etc. Before tapping JACK & JILL on the shoulders who see the ghost scream and run off)

NELLIE: *(Noticing Jack & Jill have gone)* Jack & Jill have gone!

WILL, ROBIN & NELLIE: Oh no!

WILL: What took them? *(audience: a ghost?)*

NELLIE: A what? *(audience: a ghost?)*

WILL, ROBIN & NELLIE: A ghost?! Well, we'll have to sing it again then won't we! Woo!

Song Eight A

(Two ghosts come on behind them and start waving etc. Before tapping ROBIN on the shoulders who sees the ghost screams and run off)

NELLIE: *(Noticing ROBIN has gone)* Robin's gone!

WILL & NELLIE: Oh no!

WILL: What took him? *(audience: a ghost?)*

NELLIE: A what? *(audience: a ghost?)*

WILL & NELLIE: A ghost?! Well, we'll have to sing it again then won't we! Woo!

Song Eight B

(Three ghosts come on behind them and start waving etc. Before tapping WILL on the shoulders who sees the ghost screams and run off)

NELLIE: *(Noticing WILL has gone)* Will's gone! Oh no! What took him? *(audience: a ghost?)* A what? *(audience: a ghost?)* A ghost?! Well, I'll have to sing it again then won't I! Woo!

Song Eight C

(Four ghosts come on behind NELLIE and start waving etc. They surround NELLIE two ghosts either side of her NELLIE looks at the ghosts on her right then on her left and then forward. The ghosts scream and run off)

NELLIE: Charming!

(Blackout)

SCENE THREE

THE SHERIFF OF NOTTINGHAM'S LAIR

Song Nine – MARION

(Enter ROBIN followed by the MERRY MEN, NELLIE, JACK and JILL)

MARION: Robin! I knew you'd come!

ROBIN: I was never going to leave you with that horrible Sheriff!

WILL: How are you all feeling? *(Audience: Merry!)*

MARION: *(Noticing JACK & JILL)* And you rescued Jack and Jill as well!

ROBIN: There's no time to lose, let's get you out of here-

MARION: Wait I've got a plan. Leave me here-

NELLIE: I'm going to level with you here Marion, that is a terrible plan-

MARION: That's not my entire plan Nellie!

NELLIE: Thank goodness for that for a second there I thought you'd lost the plot

WILL: Oh, we lost that ages ago.

MARION: At the town fayre tomorrow, there is an archery contest

ROBIN: I'm incredible with a bow and arrow!

MARION: That's part of the plan. The Sheriff won't be able to resist showing off to everyone at the town fayre, so I'll get him to enter the contest and if he wins, I'll tell him that I'll marry him.

NELLIE: Still doesn't sound like a great plan-

MARION: No but Robin will of course win the contest!

WILL: But how will Robin win if the Sheriff spots him, he'll surely have him arrested!

ROBIN: I'll go in disguise!

MARION: Great idea! I can hear the Sheriff coming, quick everybody hide!

(Everyone apart from MARION hides in ridiculous places, a lampshade on the head, behind a newspaper pretending to be statues etc)

SHERIFF: Ah, Marion my beautiful wife! Have you had enough time to think about my offer?

MARION: I have and my answer is yes, but only on one condition. You must prove your love for me!

SHERIFF: How will I do this? Would you like to see me perform a test of strength? Or perhaps an IQ test I'm very clever you know-

MARION: No. You must win the archery contest tomorrow at the town fayre

SHERIFF: Ha! Easy. I'm the greatest shot in all the land! Fine I will win the archery contest and when I do, I will marry you in front of everyone as part of the Town Fayre festivities.

MARION: As you wish… My love!

(Exit SHERIFF. Everyone comes out from their hiding places. SHERIFF walks back in everyone instantly hides again)

SHERIFF: So sorry forgot my bow and arrow! Until tomorrow my future wife! *(Exit SHERIFF)*

(Everyone comes out from their hiding places again)

ROBIN: We'll see you tomorrow, Marion! And after tomorrow the Sheriff will get his comeuppance and we shall all live happily ever after!

WILL: Brilliant! Now let's get out of here before the Sheriff comes back!

(Exit all apart from MARION)

Song Ten – MARION

(Blackout)

SCENE FOUR

SHERWOOD MARKET

Song Eleven – FAIRY and Company

FAIRY: So today is the day
It's the town fayre hip-hooray!
Marion's plan is all in place
So, keep your eyes peeled and watch this space
And yes, I'm back to rhyme once more
Speaking normally if I'm honest was quite a bore
I'll be keeping watch I say
Making sure that good can win the day!

(Enter the MERRY MEN)

TOWN CRIER: Ladies and Gentlemen, boys and girls welcome to the world-famous Sherwood Town Fayre! It's time for your Sherwood Fayre entertainment for the day. So, without further ado please bring up the lights and welcome to the stage the world-famous Balloon Ballet!

(Enter NELLIE & WILL both dressed in Tutus)

WILL: How are you all feeling? *(Audience: Merry!)*

Routine – The Balloon Ballet – NELLIE & WILL (the Balloon Ballet should end with the Balloon popping)

TOWN CRIER: Ladies and Gentlemen, Boys and Girls give it up for the world-famous Balloon Ballet! Now prepare yourselves for delight and mystery all the way from the Pyramids of Egypt, performing live it's the Merry Egyptian Sand Dancers!

Routine – Sand Dance – NELLIE, WILL, ALAN, JOHN and TUCK

TOWN CRIER: And now for the amazing vocal talents of Sherwood's very own Friar Tuck, please welcome to the stage the Friar of Swing!

Song Twelve – TUCK

(During Tuck's song, NELLIE realises she has lost a small bag of gold, NELLIE, WILL, ALAN and JOHN begin looking for it onstage and during the song end up in the audience looking for the small bag of gold, causing utter chaos in the audience going through different lines of seats, getting the audience to move so

they can have a look under their seats, causing as much mayhem as possible during Tuck's number, TUCK however carries on with his song regardless of what is happening. Just as the song is finishing NELLIE realises, she had the small bag of gold in her pocket all along. WILL, ALAN, JOHN and NELLIE get back to the stage just as Tuck's song is finishing)

NELLIE: *(Just as the song is finishing)* He should have had a bigger part. *(Exit NELLIE)*

(Song finishes)

TOWN CRIER: Give it up for the fantastic Friar Tuck what a great way to start our festivities! Coming up soon we'll be having the annual archery contest!

TUCK: I'm so nervous about today, what if something goes wrong? We've all had it!

ALAN: I'm sure Robin has it all in hand!

JOHN: Yes, I believe this plan is fool proof!

WILL: Hang on where's my Mum gone?

TUCK: I know what to do! Hey, look over there isn't that a lovely looking trifle! *(The MERRY MEN all sneak towards the trifle)*

(Enter NELLIE)

NELLIE: Who's trying to take my trifle! Oh, I might have known it was you lot again!

TUCK: It's honestly the quickest way to get you onstage… I mean here… to the town fayre.

TOWN CRIER: Hear ye, hear ye! Let it be known it is now time for the annual Sherwood Archery competition. Where this year's prize is Maid Marion's hand in marriage!

(Enter MAID MARION waving to the crowd)

TOWN CRIER: Hear ye, hear ye! Contestants of this year's contest please make an orderly line ready with your bow and arrows!

(TUCK, ALAN, JOHN, NELLIE and WILL all line up ready with their bow and arrows)

TOWN CRIER: Now ladies and gentlemen, boys and girls, people of all ages please welcome to the competition last year's winner and esteemed archer the Sheriff of Nottingham!

(Enter SHERIFF)

SHERIFF: Thank you, thank you all so much for coming to watch me win again as I always do!

TOWN CRIER: Now the rules are very simple the closest arrow to the bullseye is the winner. First archer Friar Tuck please step forward.

(TUCK fires his arrow)

TOWN CRIER: Miss! Next Alan-a-Dale!

(ALAN fires his arrow. We hear a crash noise from offstage)

TOWN CRIER: Miss, though you have hit my car. Little John please step up to the mark.

(JOHN fires his arrow. The stage manager walks onstage with an arrow through their head looking very angry, they shake their head at JOHN and walk back off)

TOWN CRIER: Miss. *(The TOWN CRIER is handed a note from one of the ensemble. He reads the note aloud)* Could the owner of a red Vauxhall with the number plate C K 0 8 D C Q 4 7 D A Q R T K L O P 9 8 0 4 A Z C V B N M R Q 7 1 3 5 8 H K I S D F R T V C X Z N M L O 9 6 3 1 2 5 6 7 0 1 A B F D R T W Q P O K J Y U I P W 2 3 5 7 9 8 W R T H Q please move your vehicle as your number plate is blocking the driveway. Next up Nellie please take your position and fire when ready.

(NELLIE fires her arrow)

TOWN CRIER: Miss. But please take my number and call me later. *(Hands his number to NELLIE)*. Will Scarlet, please take your shot.

(WILL fires his arrow. The arrow is thrown back onstage from behind WILL)

TOWN CRIER: Miss. And now finally the Sheriff of Nottingham.

(SHERIFF fires his arrow)

TOWN CRIER: Bullseye!

TUCK: *(To NELLIE)* Where's Robin?

NELLIE: He'll be here!

TOWN CRIER: So, for the second year in a row the winner of the archery contest is-

(Enter ROBIN who is in disguise and putting on a different voice)

ROBIN: Hello there me old mucker might I get a go at this archery contest-

SHERIFF: Let him have a go, he's not going to get better than a bullseye!

TOWN CRIER: Very well. Step forward old man and take your shot.

(ROBIN fires his arrow)

TOWN CRIER: I don't believe it this man's arrow has split the Sheriff's arrow down the middle! We have a new winner! What is your name strange man?

ROBIN: I am no strange man for I am *(throws off disguise)* Robin Hood!

SHERIFF: Robin Hood! You stupid boy, you shouldn't have come here, on guard! *(SHERIFF draws his sword)*

ALAN: *(Throws ROBIN a sword)* Robin catch!

ROBIN: Oh no I'm not very good with a sword, I mean I'm great with a bow and arrow-

MARION: Good job I'm fantastic with a sword then! *(MARION draws her sword)*

SHERIFF: You want to fight me again? Didn't you learn your lesson from last time? You can't beat me you're just a girl!

MARION: I'll show you who's just a girl you pig headed, egotistical-

SHERIFF: Such big words-

(MARION interrupts the SHERIFF by swinging her sword at him. The SHERIFF blocks her swing with his sword. There is a sword fight between MARION and the SHERIFF. MARION wins and the SHERIFF ends up on his knees while MARION points her sword at him)

MARION: Did you really think you'd win my hand in marriage in a competition? I'd never marry such a snivelling, vile, awful, horrible human being like you! And I am certainly not a prize to be won! Now what should we do with the Sheriff everyone?

WILL: What should we do with him boys and girls?

(A mysterious man stands up from the background and takes down his hood, it is KING RICHARD)

KING: I have an idea.

(Everyone gasps saying it's the King etc. Everyone bows to the King apart from the SHERIFF)

SHERIFF: King Richard!

KING: Yes, I'm back from the crusades and I've been told all about your dastardly behaviour! You are now banished from this Kingdom and must live out the rest of your days in *(local dive)*.

SHERIFF: No please anything but that!

MARION: Now go on. Get lost! *(She puts her sword up as if to charge at the SHERIFF)*

SHERIFF: *(Running off scared)* No! Please don't hurt me!

ALL: Cheer

KING: It's good to be back!

ROBIN: It's good to have you back your majesty!

KING: Robin, I believe you have something to do.

ROBIN: *(Takes MARION'S hand and gets down on one knee)* Marion, will you marry me?

MARION: Of course I will! *(They kiss)*

TUCK: *(To NELLIE)* How about making it a double whammy! Nellie say you'll marry me.

NELLIE: Oh yes Tucky, yes a thousand times!

TUCK: I'm going to make you so happy! You're in for a lifetime of happiness and surprises!

NELLIE: Not half the surprise you'll get on our honeymoon!

WILL: Well would you look at that everyone, a happy ending!

(The action freezes. FAIRY appears)

FAIRY: And so that's the end of our tale
Where good and true did prevail
We hope you've seen that if you're mean and bad

You'll only end up alone and sad
And if your good and true
Amazing things can happen for you
Enough of me rhyming on
It's time for a party so sing a long!

Song Thirteen – All (Apart from SHERIFF)

(Blackout)

SCENE FIVE

IN FRONT OF TABS

WILL: How are you all feeling? *(Audience: Merry!)* Have you all had a good time? *(Audience: Yeah!)* Good I'm glad you've all enjoyed yourselves. Well, that was fun! Hang on a minute I might as well do it one last time! How are you all feeling! *(Audience: Merry!)*. Now let's see I think we've got a few shout outs and birthdays to celebrate *(ad lib any announcements an birthdays. If there are any birthdays sing 'Happy Birthday')*. Do you know I can't believe that trifle is still here *(moves toward the trifle. Audience: Nellie!)*

NELLIE: Who's trying to go near my trifle! Oh, Silly Willy Scarlet! Actually, I can take that trifle in now. I'm entering it into the best trifle competition at the town fayre! *(Picks up the trifle and hands it offstage)*. Now did I hear you singing, I love singing, I feel it really clears the cobwebs away!

WILL: If you start singing, you'll clear everyone away!

NELLIE: Oh, I can't believe it, a happy ending!

WILL: Robin and Marion are getting married

NELLIE: And we'll never have to see that nasty old Sheriff again! And I can't believe it I'm getting married too! Me and Tucky are going to ride off into the sunset together!

NELLIE: I'm so happy I could sing a song!

WILL: Well, that's handy because we know one!

NELLIE: Do we? Well, isn't that a stroke of luck!

WILL: Music please!

Song Fourteen – WILL & NELLIE – Songsheet

NELLIE: Oh, that was so good Will!

WILL: It was but I reckon everyone should join in!

NELLIE: Right then everyone on your feet!

WILL: And just to make sure you're all joining in we've had the words written up nice and big so you can all see them! *(the song sheet descends from the top of the stage)*

NELLIE: Right then altogether, nice and loud! Music please!

Song Fourteen A – WILL & NELLIE – Songsheet

NELLIE: Now that was good! But I think this side were louder!

WILL: Well that's funny because I thought this side, my side, were louder!

NELLIE: Well I tell you what, how about a bit of a competition, my side will go first and then yours afterwards

WILL: But who can we get to judge it?

(TUCK enters)

TUCK: I'll do it!

NELLIE: What do you reckon everyone, should we let him do it? *(Audience: Yes!) (Ad lib as needed)*

WILL: Right okay then we have our judge, you go first!

NELLIE: Very well, right, my side here we go!

Song Fourteen B – WILL & NELLIE – Songsheet

WILL: It was good, however my side let's do it even louder! *(Ad lib as needed)*

Song Fourteen C – WILL & NELLIE – Songsheet

NELLIE: So, who's the winner?

WILL: Yeah who's the winner?

TUCK: I have come to my decision and the winner is… This side! *(Pick whichever side was the loudest) (NELLIE and WILL ad lib to whatever the decision is)*

NELLIE: Right well I've got a wedding to get ready for I'll see you later on! Bye for now! *(To TUCK)* Come on you! *(NELLIE and TUCK exit)*

WILL: Well, I guess that just leaves us then! I'll tell you what let's sing it all together one last time, but this time the loudest you've ever sung it!

Song Fourteen D – WILL & NELLIE – Songsheet

WILL: See you at the wedding! Bye *(Exit WILL)*

SCENE SIX - BOWS

(Tabs open for bows)

(BOWS)

FAIRY: So that's it we're at the end our final call

TUCK: I have a wife, she's like me both broad and tall

SHERIFF: I'm exiled forever I should have been nice

JACK & JILL: Yes, you really should have thought twice

MARION: Robin and I are married and happy

ROBIN: I hope you didn't find this love story to sappy

NELLIE: Me and Tucky will be alright

WILL: This is the last thing I'll say tonight

MARION: So, whether you've come from far or near

ALL: We hope to see you all next year!

Song Fifteen – Full Company

(Final Cast Bow)

(CURTAIN)

(END)

Also by Joe Meloy and available from Beercott Books

Set in the quaint little French village of [INSERT LOCAL REFERENCE HERE!], not far from [ANOTHER LOCAL REFERENCE!] is where our tale is set. Will the Beast be able to find true love before it's too late, will our dastardly villain Lucas Luxuriant get his comeuppance? Will Fairy Dust help save the day, and will Potty Pierre and Madame Marie Macaroon be able to get dinner ready and keep the Beast from going feral? Find out in this Pantomime adventure packed with fantastic gags, slapstick and something for all the family!

Will our dashing Prince save the day? Will Dame Maisy Marmalade and Muddles be more of a help than hindrance? Are the Dwarfs actually Dwarfs? And will the #Selfie obsessed Evil Queen be stopped? Join us in the Pantomime story of Snow White & the Seven Dwarfs!

Packed out with hilarious comedy routines and of course plenty of audience participation this Panto will have the whole family laughing and asking for more! OH YES IT WILL!

Jump into the rabbit hole and join Alice in Wonderland! How mad is the Mad Hatter? Will the White Rabbit ever be on time? Did anyone actually steal the Queen of Hearts jam tarts? Alice meets Duchess Dolly Dollop and Wally the White Rabbit, as they guide Alice through Wonderland and round up all of their friends to take on the Evil Queen of Hearts and save Wonderland!

About the author

I'm Joe Meloy ('...the excellent pantomime dame...' British Theatre Guide) and I'm an Actor, Pantomime Dame, Producer and Panto Enthusiast. I attended my first Pantomime when I was three and instantly fell in love with one of the most entertaining forms of theatre, in my humble opinion of course!

I have been performing in pantomime myself for a number of years having played Widow Twankey to an Ugly Sister, there have been one or two occasions where I haven't been in the dress, but I much prefer putting on my dresses, fake eyelashes and lip stick!

I performed my first professional Pantomime at twenty-three years old playing an Ugly Sister in an adult pantomime. I returned the next year to perform as Widow Twankey, from there I went on to play in family pantomimes as; Widow Twankey (twice more!) Dame Dolly Dollop, Nurse Nellie, King Arthur and as Maid Joan for the Hazlitt Theatre.

Reviews

'Something for everyone, from young to old, the future of writing pantomime is in good hands. Funny and strong story telling make these scripts a joy'.
Hayden Parker, The Panto Podcast

'Fantastic scripts, full of strong routines and great gags! Great scripts suitable for both Am Dram and Professional productions'.
Mark James, BGT Semi Finalist, Comedy Magician & Panto Legend

'Just a like a good bowl of coco pops, this script snaps, crackles and pops with light relief and laughter from the off.'
David Zachary, Resident Comic at the Hazlitt Theatre